To Noah, Sky, and Isla. I am so proud to share you with the world — Julie Gassman

www.raintreepublishers.co.uk
Visit our website to find out
more information about
Raintree books.

To order:
☎ Phone 0845 6044371
📄 Fax +44 (0) 1865 312263
✉ Email myorders@raintreepublishers.co.uk

Customers from outside the UK please telephone +44 1865 312262

Raintree is an imprint of Capstone Global Library Limited, a company
incorporated in England and Wales having its registered office at
7 Pilgrim Street, London, EC4V 6LB – Registered company number:
6695582

First published by © Picture Window Books in 2011
First published in the United Kingdom in paperback in 2012
The moral rights of the proprietor have been asserted.

Creative Director: Heather Kindseth
Art Direction/Graphic Designer: Kay Fraser
Editor: Catherine Veitch
Originated by Capstone Global Library Ltd

ISBN 978 147476 571 8 (paperback)
21 20 19 18 17
10 9 8 7 6 5 4 3 2 1

British Library Cataloguing in Publication Data
A full catalogue record for this book is available
from the British Library.

Printed and bound in India.

Eleanor

Won't Share

written by Julie Gassman   illustrated by Jessica Mikhail

Eleanor was a sweet girl.

She really was.

But Eleanor had a problem.

A BIG problem.

Eleanor did NOT like to share.

So Eleanor made a list of rules
to make sharing easier.

1. Always share things you don't like.

2. Always share things that belong to other people.

3. Always share when it makes things more fun . . . for you!

When Eleanor got a bag of sweets,
she sorted them by colour.

She gave the black ones away and ate the rest.

"The black ones are yucky!"
Eleanor said.

Eleanor **did not like sharing** her dolls.

But she always used the dolls' clothes her friend brought over.

"I just love sharing your things,"

Eleanor said.

Eleanor never
wanted to share her bricks –
unless she needed someone to play with.

"See? Aren't you having fun sharing with me?"

Eleanor said.

At school, Eleanor tried to be nice to her classmates. She didn't mind **sharing** her treats.

"You can have my grapes," she told the boy next to her. **"I don't really like** healthy things."

She didn't mind **sharing** her painting, either.
It was always more fun to paint with a friend.

But Eleanor DID mind sharing in the home corner.

"Please **don't touch** that sparkly gown!"

"Um, I **was using** that cowboy hat."

"Excuse me, but **I need** that top for my outfit."

Eleanor knew she should share the clothes.
But according to her **sharing rules,**
she didn't have to.

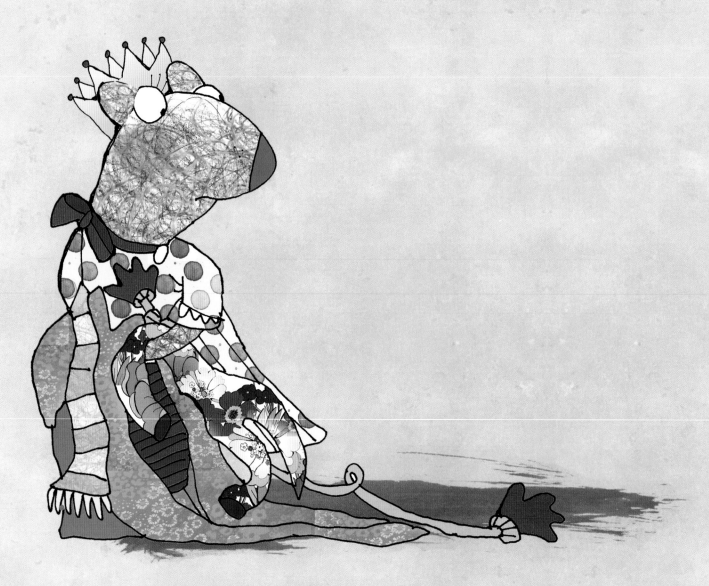

So, every day, Eleanor would take all of the
dressing-up clothes for herself.

The other children were **NOT happy** about it.

Soon, they stopped playing with the
dressing-up clothes, and with Eleanor.

One day, Miss Smith taught everyone a new game.

While Eleanor was hoarding all the dressing-up clothes,
the other children were laughing and dancing around.

Eleanor collected all the clothes and headed
over to the game.

"Can I play the new game?"

Eleanor asked. But nobody heard her.

"CAN I PLAY THE NEW GAME?"

Eleanor shouted.

This time everyone heard her,
but nobody seemed to care.

"It's not fair," Eleanor said. "You are supposed to let everyone play."

"We don't want to play with someone who doesn't share," Adam said.

"That's not very nice,"

Eleanor said.

"Neither is hoarding the dressing-up clothes," Lilly said.

Eleanor thought hard.

Then she took off
the cowboy hat.

She took off
the top, too.

And finally, she took
off the fancy gown
and crown.

The other children let her play the new game.

After class, Miss Smith whispered to Eleanor, "It's always good to share, even when you don't want to."

Eleanor whispered back, "From now on I will try to share – even when I don't want to."

"That's great!" Miss Smith said.

"Miss Smith?" Eleanor asked.

"There is something **I want to** share
with you right now."

"What's that?" asked Miss Smith.

"A hug!"